Tilly Bummie
And Other Stories

D0094038

TILLY BUMMIE
And Other Stories

Life in Jamaican Country and Town

by

Hazel Cambell

with illustrations by
Clovis Brown

LMH
Publishing

Published by
LMH Publishing Ltd.
P.O. Box 8296,
7 Norman Road,
LOJ Industrial Complex
Building 10
Kingston CSO, Jamaica
E-mail: lmhpublishing@cwjamaica.com

ISBN 976-610-235-X

Illustrations by Clovis Brown
Cover Design by Susan Anderson
Typeset by Lazertec Limited
Printed by Lightning Print

TABLE OF CONTENTS

INTRODUCTION

This book is an attempt to make up to my children for the fact that I did not find the time to tell them stories when they were little.

My mother told me stories: Anancy stories, "duppy" stories, things that happened when she was a child.

This collection is made up from bits and pieces of the stories she told me about growing up in the hills of St. Ann, as well as from my own experiences of childhood in the city of Kingston.

Of course nothing happened in the same way that I have told it and none of the characters in this book really existed in the way that I have described them. In other words the people and the situations are fictitious.

I hope that my readers will think carefully about both the positive and negative aspects of the experiences I have related.

Happy reading!

Hazel Campbell

Life in Country...

BRENTON PARK

In the 1920s nearly everybody in the district was related to everybody else. So they said.

Originally, Brenton Park had been one large estate with sugar cane, which didn't do too well up in those hills; pimento and coffee, which did considerably better; and a lot of hill-and-gully pastureland for cattle.

The founder of the village was a white man from England who had left the property to the only child anybody had called his name for. This high-mulatto son had married a high-mulatto lady and their children all looked white or nearly white in the faded pictures which still hung on the walls up at the big house. It was important to remember this. So they said.

In time, as Mr. Brenton's descendants married and had children and grandchildren, the complexion of the family changed. Only a sprinkling of high-colour throwbacks now reminded them of their cherished heritage, and the property itself was divided and sub-divided as each generation tried to give the next a little square of independence.

Gradually the estate evolved into Brenton Park district or village; people called it one or the other. It had a main road of dirt passing through what could be called its centre. This led in one direction to Brown's

Brenton Park village centre

Town, a big place with "rich big houses and shops" and a big market. Many of the children longed for the day when they would be old enough to travel the long, arduous distance to this town, a journey involving at least two days and lots of walking if one was not lucky enough to find a cart going that way, or have a donkey to ride on. Beyond Brown's Town was that marvel which some of the big people themselves had not seen. No matter that they lived on an island, few of those who lived in the village had seen the sea and the large ships which visited the harbour.

In the opposite direction, the road led to that other marvellous place called Kingston. Few of those who left by this road ever returned to Brenton Park, and some had even gone to more wondrous places with glamorous-sounding names – America, Cuba, Panama. Some of them had gone on to wars in faraway places. Letters would occasionally arrive with stories which sent the children's imaginations galloping as they tried to comprehend the strange, fantastic tales they heard.

As it passed through the village the road bulged considerably. On one side were the two or three shops which provided the commercial centre for the inhabitants. On the opposite side was the spiritual and social centre: the Anglican church with its graveyard stretching out to the community ground where fairs and socials and all large celebrations were held. Two smaller churches, the Seventh Day and the Holiness Church, were hidden on side roads.

Living in Brenton Park was like living in one large family. Now and then when a branch of the family died out, the land might be rejoined to an adjacent holding, or sometimes it was sold to an "outsider." Usually, though, new people came into the district mainly through the intimate connection of marriage or "living together."

Individual joys were shared by the whole community and quarrels were family quarrels, generally to be settled as a last resort up at the big house where lived the oldest and the mightiest of the family, Taata Bert and his wife, Miss Clara. Little Clara, who had been named for the old lady who was her great-aunt, was not sharply aware of all this history. She only knew that she had the free run of the district, getting a welcome wherever she went, sharing a meal with the

5

Shooting birds

aunts and cousins wherever mealtime happened to catch her.

To be a child in Brenton Park meant roaming the many acres of the district in packs, living off oranges, pears, guavas, fallen ripe bananas – whatever fruits were in season. Rarely would anyone stop the children from raiding the fruit trees since there was more than enough for everyone and generally only the ground provisions or the "hard food" were saved to take or send to market to get the needed cash. The children were even allowed to pick up and dry and sell their own "rat-cut" coffee, for which they would get a "smalls."

Life in Brenton Park was pleasant, especially during the long summer holidays when there was enough time to do chores and still roam the district climbing or pelting fruit trees reluctant to give up their bounty; shooting birds with catapults or bingy; splashing and swimming in the shallow river (this against adult orders, for the river had drowned Emanuel many years ago); surreptitiously tending wounds from barbed wire and "macca" which the adults would quarrel about when they were discovered, and scrub and sprinkle with "blue stone" until the tears came; or just lazing under shady trees out of the glare from the hot blue sky and the scorching sun, which by mid-August would turn the pasture grass into brown crackling paper, and dry the river to a damp spot with a slight trickle now and then, except the year of the flood when the water did more damage than the drought ever could.

Sometimes the children got summer drunk and bored with the sheer richness of the life they led.

Clara, growing up in this district, enjoyed it all. As long as there was daylight, she was happy. Her troubles began at nightfall. Generally the children tried to get home by dusk. Tired and hungry, they would stop at the nearest accommodating houses to eat and rest and sometimes even sleep over if the aunt or cousin would agree.

Night came quickly in the countryside, and then the paths, so friendly by day, became frightening. Familiar objects, trees and places took on strange, threatening shapes at night. There were unseen stones set to trip people by the "agents of darkness." Only the dim lamplight from a house here and there reminded one of the presence of people in this hostile, dark, nighttime world.

Clara, even more so than the other children, was abnormally afraid of the dark. Perhaps it was because she was an only child living alone with her mother, a rare thing in a district where families usually had twelve or more offspring.

The children all knew of her excessive fear and never lost an opportunity to tease her. They would remind her how a big ten-year-old girl like her could only walk in the dark if she was tightly clutching her mother's hand and with her eyes closed. Sometimes she fought those who teased her, but never near to nightfall, because she would have to beg for company if she found herself too far from home then.

To make matters worse, duppy stories had an unnatural attraction for her. Even the threat of near darkness couldn't budge her: if any storytelling was promised, she would linger on, eager to hear her favourite stories re-told, and sometimes if she was lucky there would be a new one which somebody had heard from somewhere.

Clara never tired of rolling-calf with his jingling bell, nor of three-foot horse whose clippety-clops had the telltale beat missing when he wandered through the village at night. The headless man, the ghost of a villager who had been murdered a very long time ago, was the most frightening of all, for people said that he still stalked the village looking for revenge, and nobody could tell where or when the ghost in his capriciousness might suddenly decide to take this revenge.

Clara listened to the stories with round, wondering eyes. She learned how the cotton tree was a favourite resting place for ghosts; how one should be careful to say a good "howdy" to anyone encountered on the road at night; how one should never ever take the short cut through the church yard at night (even in daytime this could be dangerous as a duppy could follow you home). She learned how one's head grew big, and one's feet got heavy like lead in the presence of a duppy. She was fascinated by duppy talk because the ghosts all talked up in their noses like Br'er Anancy.

Clara's favourite story was "Longer Than These Are They." This could be an almost endless tale, as each time the haunted man tried to explain to a new person he met on the road at night how horrible the duppy's teeth were, the newcomer would show his teeth asking "Longer than these?" and thus reveal himself to be the same duppy haunting the man.

Good fortune stayed with Clara for a long time as she never had to walk on the road alone at night. Knowing her great fear, the aunt or big cousin would always order some children to accompany her home if she was out too late.

"Me no want nothing happen to Miss B one pickney," they would exclaim.

But one night when Clara was sound asleep, tired from a long summer's day play in the sun, her mother awakened her. She was feeling sick and Clara had to go fetch the nearest aunt as quickly as she could.

Only the fright caused by her mother's groans and the fear that she might be dying could get Clara to be brave enough to go out into the nine o'clock, pitch-dark country night. The nearest aunt, Aunt Liza, lived half a mile away through the short cut. Even if she could run all the way, she still had to pass by Cotton

Tree Corner, the favourite resting place for duppies.

Clara stepped out fearfully into the night. Her mother had given her the lantern which she soon discovered didn't make much difference in the thick darkness. A mild fog had enveloped the area, for Brenton Park was in a hilly part of the country.

Clara stumbled along the path; sometimes she shut her eyes, but this only made matters worse as she tripped over tree roots or stones. Once when she stumbled, the lantern flew out of her hand and the light went out.

Her plight was now desperate. At any moment she expected to feel the icy hand of a ghost descending on her neck. Suppose the headless ghost chose this moment to be walking through the district? Clara began to cry.

Suddenly she remembered that duppies didn't like noise and were especially afraid of hymns. In her fright the only hymn she could remember was "Hark! The Herald Angels Sing." In a high, quavery, fear-filled voice, Clara began her Christmas song.

Just at that moment, Charlie, one of Aunt Liza's sons, was running along the path to Clara's house. His mother had sent him to find out if her sister was all right. She had a feeling, she said, that "something was wrong."

Now Charlie was a big boy, thirteen or fourteen years old, and not supposed to be afraid of the dark. Nonetheless, Charlie was taking no chances. He didn't intend to linger on the road, so he ran bird-speed along the path. Too late he heard Clara's high-pitched singing. Charlie crashed into Clara, and being sure

Charlie crashed into Clara

that it was a ghost – who else would be singing a Christmas song in August, in that high-pitched voice? – Charlie turned tail and headed back to his house faster than you could say "Howdy."

When they could quieten him enough to make sense out of the nonsense he was babbling, his mother sent the older ones to get a few more uncles and aunts and cousins. She was more than ever convinced that something was wrong.

They found Clara prostrate in the path, still in a dead faint. Nobody ever knew whether it was Charlie's weight as he charged into her which had knocked her out, or whether she had fainted from fright.

They picked her up and carried her home in time to help with the preparations to welcome her new baby sister.

And nobody ever managed to convince either Clara or Charlie that they had encountered each other, and not a duppy, on the path on that eventful night.

THE ARK

The children knew about it even before the adults began to whisper together and forbade them to go near Drinkall House.

They knew about the carryings-on of the two Drinkall sisters from Monday morning when John-John and his sister Eda on their way to school had been startled by the sight of Miss Nadia stark naked in her garden and beckoning to them wildly.

John-John and Eda had been so frightened that they had run all the way to school where the story spread from "A" class to sixth standard. Even the pupil teachers and assistant teacher heard about it, so that it was no surprise to the children when, at recess time that Monday morning, every child who went home for lunch was warned not to use the short cut which passed Drinkall House.

At dismissal time on Monday afternoon Teacher Madden, the headmaster, better known as White Shoes to the children, called the school together and repeated the warning with a threat of punishment for any child who disobeyed and walked past Drinkall House.

All of Monday evening the adults whispered together in little groups, discussing the situation at Drinkall House where the two middle-aged sisters Nadia and

They took turns watching the house

Madeline seemed to have finally gone "round the bend." A telegram had been sent to their brother who was a doctor in Kingston, but he probably wouldn't get there for a couple of days.

But while the adults speculated and tried to figure out what to do – because the sisters were too high in status for just anybody to assume authority over them, even if they had gone mad, but at the same time they couldn't just be left alone – while the adults puzzled their brains, strange tales of wild happenings at Drinkall House spread among the village children.

Although they had been forbidden to go near the house, and the adults grew quiet whenever they came near, the children knew even more about what was happening at the house than the big people did.

For one thing, they could climb trees, and from their hidden vantage points in otaheite apple, guinep, breadfruit or other large leafy trees, they would take turns reporting to those on the ground what they could see.

Sometimes there were long spells of quiet when nothing stirred in or near Drinkall House. At such times those on the ground would run off to play some other game, but these wouldn't last too long, for the expected happenings at Drinkall were not to be missed.

Sometimes loud shrieks could be heard, and the children frightened each other with highly imaginative tales of torture and death for those who had been caught by the sisters. After a time, few knew where fiction had taken control of the stories they told each other.

By bedtime on Monday night, they were satisfied that Miss Maidy and Miss Nadia had captured at least three adults and were preparing to kill them sometime during the night. After this, they theorised, they would come into the village and woe be unto anyone foolish enough to be out of his or her house at this time. The stories got mixed up with witches flying on brooms at nighttime and this made the whole thing more exciting, especially because these two witches would be naked!

It was the story of the captured adults who would be sacrificed during the night that first got them into trouble. One of the supposedly captured adults was Mas' Carpenter, Sammy's father. Sammy, who was in third standard, had helped to keep watch during the afternoon and had not seen his father enter the house. He vigorously denied that his father had been captured but the story persisted. The children didn't like Mas' Carpenter who was fond of telling tales on them and roughing them up over trivial matters. Sammy tried to ignore the story but, when one hour after he reached home his father had not yet returned from work in the field, fear grabbed him and he sob-bingly told his mother the whole story.

She in turn, although "nonsensing" Sammy's tale, was still a little worried, since Mas' Carpenter was staying out later than usual. It was with great relief that she finally saw him entering the yard. She told him Sammy's story, and he, stern disciplinarian that he was, promised to report the children to teacher Madden the following morning and have them punished.

The next morning, Tuesday, the children went to school as early as they could to discuss the situation and hear any new embellishments which might have been dreamt up during the night.

When the bell rang for morning prayers they gathered in their usual spot at the back of the schoolhouse where there was a raised earthen platform for Teacher to stand on while he addressed them. They, especially those who had broken yesterday's ruling, noticed with sinking hearts that Teacher Madden was wearing his white shoes, his white shirt, his white suit and white tie – his beating clothes – a sure sign that the cane would "talk" that day.

But, surprisingly, the session ended with only a severe warning of fire and brimstone for any of them who disobeyed the order not to go within sight of Drinkall House.

However, Teacher Madden didn't know the extent of their curiosity. Nobody had gone mad in the district before, not on such a grand scale anyway, and never anybody with such high status, for the Drinkalls were rich, high-brown "outsiders" who had bought a piece of property and settled in the district. The parents had died and the brother moved away, leaving the two old maid sisters to live off the small property as best they could.

By recess time, newer and more exciting tales buzzed around the school. The sisters, both of them, had been seen stark naked dancing on the roof of their house. Tortured shrieks and cries of help were issuing from the house minutely.

Shortly after the bell rang to announce the beginning of recess, the school yard was almost empty. There were no chasing, skipping, ring or ball games. No shrieks, no cries of excitement or anger criss-crossed the playing field as usual. If Teacher Madden had not been busy with a personal matter, the silence would have alerted him sooner and the happenings averted.

As it was, only timid souls remained at school, the very timid ones.

Some forty-odd of the sons and daughters of Brenton Park trooped along, silent with anticipation, straight into the Drinkall yard, each determined to see for himself exactly what was going on.

The stories got mixed up with witches flying on brooms

They found themselves in a disappointingly quiet yard. No naked women danced on rooftops. There were no screeches, nor cries for help. Indeed, if they didn't know for a fact that two crazy women were in the house they would have turned back in disappointment.

A quiet consultation (not quite as quiet as they thought) took place, with Big George from sixth class who had assumed leadership of the expedition choosing two to go up to the window and peep in. His choice, naturally, were Big Toe Suzie who had boxed him the week before and Mannie whose mother had complained to Teacher Madden about him bullying her own son.

Needless to say, neither victim was anxious to enter the lion's den, but the jeers of the others, none of whom wanted to be a replacement, and the cries of "coward" propelled them toward the house. They chose a window to the right of the living room whose blinds were open at the top. The rest huddled together, prepared either to join them or for sudden flight.

Centimetre by centimetre (that's slower than inch by inch) Mannie and Big Toe Suzie stumbled toward the chosen window. Somewhere between the crowd and the window, Big Toe Suzie realised that Mannie was hanging on to her with both hands. She shook him off impatiently but had to either consent to hold his hand or go forward alone, since he refused to budge without her personal protection.

Thus, hand in hand, they crept up to the window. Before they could pull themselves up to peep in, a loud cough made them cringe, but it was only one of the children overcome by nervousness.

They all crouched on the ground for a few moments to see what would happen. But nothing stirred within the house.

Gingerly, Suzie and Mannie got off the ground, pulled themselves up by the windowsill and peeped into the room.

So intent were all the others on the expected drama that they too had crept forward to within a couple yards of the sacrificial lambs without even realising it. So intent were they on watching the two at the window, that they were unprepared for the sudden opening of the door, and for the sight of Miss Maidy clad only in apron and long drawers beckoning them to enter the house.

Paralysed with fear, they stood their ground. Two or so at the back of the pack managed to summon enough strength to scamper away. The others took root.

"Enter, enter children!" Miss Maidy croaked. "You are just in time to enter the Ark before the deluge starts."

"Yes, enter!" a voice within demanded. "Here, Maidy. Use the whip. You know animals don't obey unless whipped."

Next thing they knew, Miss Maidy had a broom brandishing about them and they were being herded through the door.

"Two by two, shall they enter!" she yelled gleefully. "Welcome! Welcome to the Ark!"

"You're just in time," Miss Nadia told them wildly. She was sitting in a rocking chair doing needlework.

" 'For yet seven days, and I will cause it to rain upon the earth forty days and forty nights'," she exclaimed in a churchy voice. "Shut the door firmly, Maidy, for the seven days have passed and the animals are in and the rains will start at any moment. 'And those outside, every living substance, will be destroyed from the face of the earth'." She ended her speech with a loud shrieking laugh.

There are different accounts about what happened after that, but the main story line says that Miss Maidy, bare-breasted, took charge.

"Now then," she said, "we must divide up. We can't have all the animals living in the same room. Two by two," she said repeatedly and went among them trying to separate the children who were huddling together for protection.

Caroline from third standard was crying loudly. Afterwards they heard that several second standard children had wet themselves. First standard held on to each other and some little ones who had no business there wouldn't be separated.

"Well, you can be the clean beasts staying together by sevens," she twinkled at them.

"Now," Miss Maidy continued. "Food! No need to fret, children. We received warning in time. There's plenty of hay and bananas and goodies for all of us. Enough for forty days of rains," she croaked.

Nobody knew how long they had been in the Ark shivering with anxiety and fear when a loud knocking on the front door startled them all.

"Open this door!"

It was with great relief that the children recognised Teacher Madden's voice.

"The Ark is closed," Miss Nadia shouted gleefully from the rocking chair. "Those who are out must remain outside. The flood shall sweep you away. You are lost forever. You shall be destroyed from the face of the earth!"

The banging got louder and the voice angrier.

"Open this door at once, or I'll break it down."

"Perhaps we had better let him in," Miss Maidy said to her sister. "He does sound anxious to be saved from the flood."

21

One heavy push on the door released the bolt which was not very strong and Teacher Madden came charging into the room. He was so angry that at first he couldn't talk. The stories would later tell how his bottom lip trembled like liver waiting to go into the pot, but the children had never been so happy to see anyone in their entire lives.

Teacher Madden looked around and, catching sight of Miss Maidy's bare breasts, without a word took off his jacket and placed it around her shoulders.

Then he turned to the children and issued his orders. "March!" he barked. "Two by two! Straight to school!"

Hastily the children tumbled through the door. This was the weirdest sight of all to have happened at Drinkall House. Teacher Madden in his white shirt-sleeves and white tie, blowing like a bull, following a line of relief-drunk children.

So they returned to the schoolhouse. Teacher Madden didn't even bother to put on his other white jacket. A dozen new canes were lined up on his table and the pupil teachers were hastily cutting tamarind whips to supplement the canes.

It is said that after that historic beating session Teacher's arm was so sore he didn't beat anybody for a month.

For years afterwards, long after the Drinkall sisters were both dead, the house locked up and fallen into ruins, the story of the Ark would enliven many a cold, wet country evening. For those who had entered the Ark never tired of telling their children and grandchildren their particular version of the events of that exciting day.

TILLY BUMMIE

The ultimate insult was to tell a girl that she "favour Tilly Bummie."

It could mean that she adjusted her slip by hauling up the straps and tying knots which always showed and which were always dirty. It could mean that she had yellow, uneven teeth, an ugly perpetual scowl or that she wore dirty slippers on dirty feet.

But most of all it meant that she was mean-dispositioned, bad-tempered, sometimes foulmouthed, hypocritical and just plain unpleasant.

Tilly Bummie was an "outsider" in the district. She had lived with one of the village uncles until his death. They had had no children so now she lived alone, in a small ramshackle house on the slope just below the school yard where the children played. This was unfortunate because it was impossible to play cricket, kickings, softball, or any game which used a ball without that ball sooner or later finding itself into Tilly Bummie's yard.

The children would watch in dismay as a cricketer's six soared downhill and into Tilly Bummie's yard.

The balls were never returned. Not those made from wrapping and twisting "whis-whis," nor those made from carefully collected rags sewn together, nor

– a catastrophic event – those borrowed, usually without permission, from the school's meagre stock, genuine rubber balls carefully preserved for official sporting events.

The children would beg and plead across the barbed wire fence which separated the school yard from hers.

"Please, Miss Ferguson," (that was her real name) "please, we can get back the ball to finish the game?"

"Please, Miss Ferguson, we just borrow the ball, and Teacher gwine lick we."

"Please, Miss Ferguson, it tek one whole week fi mek that ball."

She never answered them. Disappointed, they would turn away, and as soon as they were out of earshot they would begin to chant in derision:

> *"Tilly Bummie*
> *nyam the ball*
> *Tilly Bummie*
> *get a fall*
> *bruk her leg*
> *an' tek to bed."*

They could never work out how she always managed to be in her yard at playtime. They couldn't even climb through the fence to retrieve the balls.

It was bad enough to face Teacher's wrath at the lost balls they had "borrowed," but it was worse when Tilly Bummie complained to Teacher about them. She did this at least once each week, confirming their suspicion that she hated them all.

"Ketch the ball, ketch it quick!"

On the days when Tilly Bummie was feeling particularly spiteful the following drama would occur:

Children's voices:
>Ketch the ball, ketch it quick! See how you mek it gone over Tilly Bummie.

Voice from Tilly Bummie's yard:
>Jesus Christ! Them lick out mi yeye.
>
>*or*
>
>Gawd! Mi dead! Them lick mi inna mi head.

Then the children would dejectedly crawl away from the playing field trying to pretend innocence; all in vain, as they knew.

They would hear Tilly Bummie wailing from her yard all the way to Teacher Madden's cottage. Those who were bold enough to look could see Tilly Bummie holding the supposedly injured place on her body. Gradually the wailing would subside and soon the bell would ring signalling the end of playtime, earlier than usual. They would line up to go into the school-house. Teacher Madden would be at the door, dressed in his white shirt, white pants and white shoes, along with the pupil teachers carrying canes or tamarind switches.

Teacher would lecture them on the consequences of carelessness and disobedience. How many times had he told them not to play ball near Miss Ferguson's house? From then on all ball playing on the school premises was forbidden!

Then, in order to enter the schoolhouse, each child would have to endure four or so licks with cane or switch. Teacher would beat until sweat poured down his face and soaked his white shirt, but he would rock on his feet with satisfaction when the last lick had been administered and the crying and whimpering testified that once more he had done his duty by these wayward children.

For a day or two afterwards, strict vigilance would be kept by the monitors and pupil teachers and the playing field would be moderately quiet at playtime. No cheers as a wicket was taken. No ball games, only the relatively quiet, sedate ring games or chasings, mostly played by the girls while the boys sulked or joined in reluctantly, for nothing could replace the vigour, the excitement, the nerve-tingling joy of a ball game.

Tilly Bummie

But before the week was finished, things would be back to normal. A new ball or two, ingeniously devised from bamboo root, rags or twine, would once again appear; vigilance relaxed in no time at all, the children would soon be back at the fence pleading, "Please, Miss Ferguson."

Generations of children passed through Brenton Park school, fearing, hating and jeering Tilly Bummie.

It was said that she piled the balls under her bed, and that the pile was now so high that it lifted the mattress, making her so uncomfortable that she couldn't sleep, and that this made her more miserable by day.

When they were much older, long after they had left school, those who had suffered because of her, would learn that the complaints and the once-a-week visit to Teacher Madden were Tilly Bummie's method of getting a shilling or two, as Teacher was obliged to compensate her for her injuries, imagined or real.

Then one day, it seemed that the accumulated evil chants had their desired effect. Tilly Bummie did fall down and break her leg, and became bedridden after that.

At first the children couldn't believe their good fortune.

No more Tilly Bummie eating up their balls.

The first girl who came to look after Tilly Bummie would eagerly throw back the balls to them, glad of a chance to participate even peripherally in their play. They could sometimes hear Tilly Bummie screaming curses at them from her house, but they didn't care. She could no longer climb the hill to complain to Teacher and get them into trouble.

The second girl didn't return the balls, but she pretended not to see the children when they crawled through the fence to retrieve the wayward balls.

One day at morning prayers, Teacher Madden made a strange announcement. Miss Ferguson, as they all knew, had been ill for some time. She was an old woman and perhaps she didn't have much longer to live. She had requested that some of the children visit her. He had decided that they should go that morning.

Needless to say, when he asked for volunteers, no hand went up. Eventually he settled the matter by choosing three children each from Standard Three to Standard Six; twelve in all with two pupil teachers to accompany them.

With heavy hearts, the representatives entered Tilly Bummie's one-room house. The room smelled of old age, sickness and stale urine.

They could hardly believe their eyes. There was Tilly Bummie, the mighty one, lying in her bed, looking frail and quite unlike the frightening figure which had terrorised them for so long. She seemed to be asleep when they reluctantly crowded into the room, those in front being pushed by those behind.

When she opened her eyes and realised who they were, a bit of her old fire returned, momentarily.

"Oonu lick any ball inna mi yard today?" she screamed at them.

"No, Miss Ferguson," they chorused politely.

"Ah!" she exclaimed. "Oonu gi' the old lady a hard time. Oonu know that?" she enquired.

When they didn't answer she continued. "Oonu lick out mi yeye them, an' batter, batter mi all 'bout

They could hardly believe their eyes

with oonu ball them. An' don't think ah didn't hear when oonu a sing say mi fall down and bruk mi leg.

"Well, see there, oonu satisfy? Mi fall down bruk mi leg. Mi, a old woman," she said, and began to cry.

And as she wept a feeling of remorse and sadness began to sweep the children, embarrassing them because they didn't know what to say or do.

A foul smell came from the trunk

"But," she continued, "ah forgive oonu. Mi soon dead. Mi can't go to God with a grudge.

"Look!" she pointed at an old trunk in a corner of the room. "Lif the trunk and tek back oonu things."

One of the pupil teachers went across to the trunk while the children looked on puzzled and slightly afraid. Then they all gazed speechless at the sight which met their eyes.

The trunk was packed with balls of all sizes and descriptions. A foul smell came from the trunk, because many of the imprisoned balls were in various stages of decay.

"Tek them away," she ordered. "Never say that Tilly

Bummie dead and gone with oonu things. Ah can't tek them with mi."

Long after Tilly Bummie's death, the stories would enlarge the incident and succeeding generations would hear how Tilly Bummie had "confessed" to many sins before the children on her deathbed.

Be that as it may, one thing was sure: for that last set of children who had played ball in fear of Tilly Bummie's wrath, a little of the zest of the games went away with her death and the absence of challenge from the locked-up desolate house below the school yard.

MATHILDA'S DAY

Mathilda was chubby from birth.

From a chubby baby she grew into a chubby child, fat you might even call her. At eight years she was fat and a bother to all her brothers and sisters and cousins who had to take care of the smaller ones, particularly at times of play or jollification, at fair or church social, tea party, or worse, first of August celebrations.

For one thing, Mathilda couldn't run and play with the other children, she was too fat and clumsy. She fell over things and people, and she was always sniffling because somebody was teasing her – "clumsy fatty bum-bum" was their favourite name for her. She couldn't walk any distance either, because she perspired so much that her legs chafed easily and she would start to cry and somebody would have to stay with her as she couldn't go any further. Mathilda was a nuisance.

Eventually, the others worked out a strategy to deal with her, since they couldn't object to taking her with them as this would mean that they would all be deprived of the outing.

If they had to walk any great distance they would divide the group into two. There were always eager-beavers anxious to reach where they were going, and

33

She longed to run about like the other children

there were always slowpokes who liked to linger over their walk, stopping to play or rest. Mathilda was put with the second group, which made it easier for her to keep up. When they reached their destination, they would park her at a convenient spot and put her in charge of the baggage – food, extra clothing for the small ones, whatever their parents might have given them to take along. This way she had to stay in one spot. If she objected they would promise her an ice cream or a sweetie, later!

But Mathilda wasn't happy. She longed to run about, light as a feather like the other children. She yearned to be able to skip; to climb trees; swing wildly from the dripping roots of the banyan tree; to play catchings and to bat a ball away into the distance. None of the children would pick her on a side, no matter how short they were.

Mathilda didn't like being left behind always to be among the slowpokes and babies. She didn't like how they teased her. Most of all she resented it when they told her that she "favoured" Aunty Zelda who was so large that Aunty's father, the Taata at the big house, would say derisively, "Her behind big like the governor washing tub."

Sometimes the children would call her "little governor washing tub," and since she couldn't fight, she had to be content with tears and an occasional complaint to an adult.

Mathilda was forced to learn other than physical ways to protect herself. "Telling on them" was one way. Then, because she spent so much time on the sidelines looking on, she learnt many little secrets about the others, things they would much rather keep from the adults. Mathilda blackmailed them quite effectively with her knowledge of these secrets.

But she wasn't happy. Her unhappiness became worse the year she was turning nine. Shortly before her birthday, which would pass unnoticed like those of all the other children in the village, the first of August would be celebrated.

The whole district had discussed nothing but the plans for the holiday for weeks. Children were busy practising recitations and songs and dances for the concert which always ended the day's festivities.

Mathilda's little brother Sammy was particularly proud of the recitation the "B" class children had learned.

All day he practised:

> *"Yittety yap to Washington,*
> *Yittety yap to Rome,*
> *Yittety yap to London Town and*
> *Yittety yap back home."*

– while running around as if he held the reins of a horse.

Night after night the village band could be heard practising the various tunes they would play to keep feet tapping and heads nodding throughout the day. Fife and banjo, drum and shaka-shaka, and jollification for the first of August were never thought of as "sinful," no matter how condemned they were the rest of the time. Adults who at other times would frown and scold threateningly at any "wild" behaviour, smiled indulgently at the children's antics. It was as if special licence was granted for this celebration of emancipation from slavery. Those who had never experienced its trauma celebrated their freedom with joyful fervour.

Brenton Park's celebrations were widely known and people would travel from other districts to gather on the village common under bamboo tents or in the open, dancing, eating, drinking, gossiping, with perhaps

36

Not even the Christmas bazaar was quite like this

a little quarrelling or fighting easily discouraged by those not involved.

It was a time to renew acquaintances, to catch up on happenings outside the district. Not even the Christmas church bazaar was quite like this.

Brenton Park knocked itself out preparing for the day, as if it had to copy slavery's state of tiredness in order to better appreciate the joy of the festivities. People saved their money for months just to be able to splurge on that day.

Night after night, Mathilda would hear her mother, who sewed for the district, labouring at her newfangled acquisition – a foot-pedal Singer sewing machine – for every woman and girl wanted a bright new dress for the occasion. Flounces and frills for the girls, long sweeping skirts for the older women. The tailor sewed clothes for the men, shoes were repaired or new ones ordered from the shoemaker. Pigs and goats and chickens earmarked for food were given special attention so that they would be fat for the killing.

The hustle and bustle which preceded the day can hardly be described.

Wet sugar from the village mill was poured by the gallon into shut pans. All sorts of goodies, marmalade, jams and jellies were made from guavas, oranges and other fruits. Dry coconuts yielded oil and more sweets and many different kinds of cakes and puddings were baked. As the day neared, the children thought they would go crazy with the excitement of it all. They were invited to taste and fit clothes and run errands in a spate of activity which transformed the usually tranquil village into one giant hum of sensual pleasure.

Mathilda had set her heart on getting a new dress for the occasion, one with frills or at least a flounce or two instead of the neat tucks and pleats which she was always given to help "keep down her size." But she knew from bitter experience that while her mother would kill herself sewing for all the district, her own children would have to wait, and sometimes did not get their clothes finished until after the event.

"The nearer the church, the farther from God," she would tell them with a sigh.

But this time, to Mathilda's joy, her dress was finished the night before the big day and though it didn't have frills at least there was a flounce which twirled out about her when she spun around, even in her clumsy way.

The John Canoe dancers came from Hatfield

Like all the children, she woke up on the first of August full of excitement, eagerly anticipating the day's events. She was so excited, she could hardly drink her tea. The other children had been talking about nothing else for weeks, so that even the events that she could not remember very well had now come alive in her imagination.

She could imagine the large common filled with the villagers and their visitors in their brightly coloured clothes, children mixing with adults, eating, drinking, dancing with joyous abandon.

She could see the maypole with its bright streamers and hear the village band playing the lively tunes as the girls and boys and adults too, did the various intricate dances which filled her with envy and the increased longing to be light on foot and agile.

She could see the John Canoe dancers who always came from Hatfield, the next district, since Brenton Park didn't have a band of its own. She could hear the sweetness of the band's fife and feel the terror of horse-head breathing on her and hear the shrieks of the children as they ran away from devil and patches, colourful, sweating and smelling of rum.

And the part she liked best was the pomp and ceremony of the opening session in the morning, when Taata Bert and Miss Clara would arrive in their buggy. The horses would be decorated with flowers and Taata would have on his high hat and flyaway coat and Miss Clara would wear a wide hat, and they would both look like Mr. and Mrs. Queen as they came down out of the buggy and went into the main tent where Taata would say something about "this memorable day" and wish them "great happiness and prosperity." Then everybody would clap and this was the signal for the jollification to begin in earnest.

Mathilda wasn't quite sure about the history of the day, something to do with slavery being abolished and freedom. What she did know was that this first of August she was determined not to be left behind by the bigger ones. Even with the added discomfort of her button-side shoes, she would be right up front with the bigger, faster ones this year because she didn't want to miss anything.

It was customary to send the children along early to help set up stalls and display goods for sale since people came to buy as well as to sell and to share what they had. Mathilda was also determined not to be left "looking after the things" as usual. This year she would walk about and play and have a good time. So, bright and early along with her brothers and sisters, she bathed and dressed herself, pleased with the newness of her dress and button-side shoes even if the straps cut into her feet because they were a little too short to comfortably meet across her fat.

Mathilda lived at one of the farthest points from the common. As usual, her brothers and sisters divided up the group which would be swollen with other children as they went along, and told her to stay with the younger, slower ones. Mathilda, however, objected strenuously, and when they resisted she threatened to "tell" one of Edward's particularly painful secrets – a love letter to the assistant teacher. So he, the eldest, had to let her start out with them.

But Mathilda needed more than courage and dreams to keep up with them that day. Eager as they were to reach the common, some of them even took off their shoes so that they could walk faster. In no time at all, they had outdistanced Mathilda. To make matters worse, the younger group soon caught up with her. And, as was usual, not only had the excitement and effort of fast walking wearied her, but her legs were chafed and burning where they rubbed together when she moved. Then Mathilda found that neither tears nor threats could gain her any sympathy. Soon the younger ones had left her too, and wave after wave of children laughingly called out to her as they skipped, hopped, ran or walked past. Even the adults who came upon her stopped only to encourage her to

41

Finally, Mathilda sat down and began to cry

continue walking; everybody was much too busy and the animals too laden to give her a ride.

Finally, still a little distance from the common, Mathilda sat down and began to cry. She had never felt so miserably uncomfortable as she did that first of August morning.

Then suddenly around a corner came the clip-clopping of the special horses pulling the buggy which always carried Taata Bert and Miss Clara.

Mathilda gazed at the splendid animals with sad tear-filled eyes. She looked so miserable and unhappy sitting on a stone by the roadside in her bright blue dress, dripping sweat and tears, that Taata Bert was touched. He was travelling alone that day for Miss

She could not believe her good fortune

Clara was ill, too ill to attend the opening ceremony with him, for the first time in many years. He also was feeling unhappy and uncomfortable without his wife beside him. He ordered the driver to stop and sent him to invite Mathilda to join him in his buggy. He had wisely summed up her distress. Didn't he also have a daughter "big as the governor washing tub"?

Mathilda could not believe her good fortune, to arrive at the common in a buggy, seated beside that great man, the Taata!

The driver reluctantly helped her up into the buggy. He liked things to go properly, and carrying a fat little girl in the buggy to the opening ceremony was not "proper" to his mind.

Mathilda was so happy she couldn't say a word. She wished they could have been farther away so she could have passed more people on the way. She loved the way the people waved and shouted "Morning, Taata," "Howdy, sah," and then stared at her sitting beside him in stately splendour. Taata Bert had lent her his handkerchief to dry her tears and sweat.

So Mathilda arrived in great splendour at the first of August celebration. Taata Bert invited her to sit beside him on the platform and she smiled sweetly at the dumbfounded children who came to stare at her in her moment of glory on Emancipation Day.

Life in Town...

SYLVIE IN TOWN

Sylvie stood on the piazza in downtown Kingston tightly clutching her suitcase, and anxiously glancing every now and then at the crocus bag of ground provisions at her feet while trying desperately to hold back the tears stinging her eyes and the fright dancing around in her head.

Sylvie had reached Kingston, the wonderful Kingston she had heard so much about, and it was even bigger and more frightening than she had ever imagined.

The many buses parked in the square, the constant arrival and departure of others, the bustling crowds doing various kinds of shopping confused her so that she could hardly stand upright.

The stores! Rows of them packed with more things than she could ever dream. The sellers on the sidewalk with trays full of beautiful fruits – apples and grapes they must be, because that was what they were shouting.

Aunt Rosa had warned her to stay quietly and guard her things while she went to see a man in the park.

Suppose she didn't return? was the most frightening thought repeating itself in Sylvie's head. She didn't even know where in Kingston she would be staying.

Kingston was bigger and more frightening than she had imagined

Aunt Rosa had said something about a place called Kencot but she didn't know if this was an address. Maybe it was a district like in the country, but she didn't even know the name of the lady with whom she would be staying. Aunt Rosa had called her Miss Betty, a nice lady who was going to take good care of her if she behaved herself and made herself useful in the house. In return she would get some pocket money and perhaps be sent to school to learn something.

"Peanuts, nice chile?" a vendor approached her.

Sylvie shook her head and smiled, a frightened smile. Aunt Rosa had warned her not to have anything to do with any stranger who approached her, for this was Town where everybody was wicked and bad.

"Nice ribbon for your hair, country girl," another said, showing her a tray of hair clips, hair nets, ribbons, thread and needles.

Sylvie shook her head and clutched her grip even tighter. Where, oh where was Aunt Rosa? And how did they know she was a country girl?

Aunt Rosa had said something like that as they journeyed into Kingston on the country bus. Funny how she had changed from a friendly, laughing person at home in the country to a miserable, complaining person the closer they got to Kingston.

In the country she had been all smiles with Sylvie's mother, assuring her that Sylvie would be all right. That the lady she was going to would take good care of her.

But on the way she had started to criticise Sylvie's clothes.

"How you frock so big fi you, girl? As they see you in town them know you come from country."

"Mek you madda have fi gi' you this big crocus bag a food?" she asked as they put the things in a handcart. "She mus' be think you gwine starve. Them bus conductor don't like carry them kinda load. Is not like country bus, you know."

Sylvie had remained quiet, but at one point had summoned up enough courage to ask if they would drive on a tramcar. Her mother had told her about them. How they were bright yellow and ran on train lines on the ground, but they were open on all sides with benches for seats and if you didn't hold on tight you could drop out as they rocked from side to side when they were going fast, and how they made plenty noise, bang-a-lang-a-lang, as they raced through the streets. Sylvie hoped she would ride on one, but when she asked, Aunt Rosa laughed at her.

"Tramcar stop run long time, from the forties. Is modern time now. Chi-chi bus time. Tramcar is ole time things."

After that Sylvie had kept quiet.

Looking about her now, she could understand why Aunt Rosa called them chi-chi bus. When they stopped and the doors opened they made a hissing sound like a boiling pot letting off steam and it sounded like chi-chi-chi.

Sylvie envied the people around her who seemed so sure of themselves. Everybody seemed to know exactly what to do, which bus to take, who to stop and talk to. Oh it was too confusing, she would never be able to cope with town life!

Just as she was about to burst into tears she heard Aunt Rosa.

"Wake up, Sylvie. Look lively. See a empty bus here. Quick, we take it before it full up and the conductor won't tek we on with the load.

"But stop! Is you me talking to, girl. Stop look like frog a wait fi ketch fly, an' pick up you things."

Sylvie struggled as best she could, grip in one hand, crocus bag in the other, holding down her head so that the breeze wouldn't blow off her hat. A picture of misery, she followed Aunt Rosa, who, after a brief argument with the bus conductor, helped her to drag the crocus bag to the back of the bus, seated herself across from Sylvie and then seemed to forget her.

Sylvie thought that this was how you had to look

when you lived in town. As if nothing interested you. She marvelled how nobody greeted anybody else when they got on the bus. How unfriendly everybody looked minding their own business.

She wondered at the way the bus drove off smoothly, not jerking up everybody like the country bus. She gawked at the large buildings crowding each other, lining the streets as they drove along. At how the bus stopped and continued the journey with only the ping of a bell as a guide.

She hoped Aunt Rosa knew where they were going because she would die of fright if they got lost.

But of course she knew, Sylvie reasoned. She had been living in town for many years.

Another long stop in another large square with lots of other buses parked in a line. She didn't know where she was as the conductor on this bus didn't announce the stops the way they did in the country. Ulster Spring! Christiana! Spauldings! Frankfield! Chapelton! May Pen! On the way to Kingston she could always tell the name of the town or village where they stopped.

Sylvie looked through the window anxiously, and, mindful of Aunt Rosa sitting across from her, she tried not to stare. But it was all so strange. There was a very large white building with a sign which said CARIB. There were all sorts of signs above the buildings. Some of them she could hardly read for the letters were too pretty.

More vendors trying to sell things through the windows; sweets, chocolates, peanuts, asham; some politely, others roughly as if threatening her.

51

Some of the signs she could hardly read

Would she ever get used to this place?

Finally, a short distance from this last long stop, Aunt Rosa signalled her.

"Get youself together, girl. Next stop is ours." Then she put up her hand, pulled a cord, and Sylvie heard the ping of the bell.

She tried to be quick, dragging grip and crocus bag past staring unfriendly eyes with the conductor saying impatiently, "Hurry up! Hurry up!"

"Is a good thing we not going far," Aunt Rosa said. "Me don't know why you mother load you up so." And, offering no help, she led the way.

After a while when she noticed Sylvie struggling to keep up with her, she sighed and said, "Why you don't put the bag 'pon you head?"

Then she helped Sylvie to settle the crocus bag on her head. Accustomed to this, Sylvie was better able to manage by keeping the load steady with one hand and carrying the grip with the other.

Thus she arrived at Miss Betty's house in Kencot, much to the amusement of Miss Betty's two children who stared at her, whispered together, laughed and ran away.

* * *

"You write your mother yet?"

"No, ma'am."

"Then you don't think she wondering what happen to you? One month since you come to town and you don't write to say that you all right?"

"Yes, ma'am."

"How you mean, yes ma'am? When you finish this evening just sit down and write her, you hear!"

"Aunt Rosa did say she gwine write her," Sylvie mumbled.

"I don't business with that. You know the market where we buy food on Saturdays in Cross Roads? Well, the post office on the other side. When you go to shop again buy some writing paper and an envelope and buy a penny stamp and then post the letter. You hear me!"

"Yes, ma'am."

One month since she had come to town! What to tell her mother?

Dear Mama, I reach safe. The lady nice and the children nice and the place nice. I get plenty food and everything alright. Yours faithfully, your daughter, Sylvie.

How to tell her mother how lonely it was to have nobody to talk to but the two children who laughed at everything she said, and constantly called her foolish because there were so many things she didn't know?

Would Mama understand how horrible it was to live in an outhouse separate from the rest of the family? At night when she had finished working she bathed and crawled into the bare little room and locked the door tight. Even with the electric light she still was afraid.

Would Mama understand how many things she had to learn to do which were different from home?

"Light the stove, Sylvie, and put on the kettle."

"Yes, ma'am." But since she didn't know what to do she just stood there, one foot rubbing the other, until anger broke over her head.

She just stood there, one foot rubbing the other

"What you doing standing there? I tell you to light the stove. The water should be boiling already."

"Yes, ma'am," the tears threatening to spill over.

"Oh, of course. I forget. You don't know what to do. Then why you don't say so. How you going to learn if you don't open your mouth and ask question. Lord have mercy! I'm going to have to teach you everything from scratch. And all of you so ungrateful. As soon as you learn you find a man to go off with or somebody who offer to pay more.

"You just look. Lift up this part like this, after you

make sure that enough kerosene oil in the bottle. Then you light it like this and adjust the flame. You understand?"

"Yes, ma'am."

But she just couldn't get it right so that the flame was always too high and the pots always got blackened and the lady was always quarrelling.

But that wasn't all.

"You mean to tell me that you clean the bathroom! Look at this ring in the tub. What you say you do any at all!"

"These clothes don't start wash yet. Look at Mr. Edward shirt collar!"

"Yes, ma'am."

"No, ma'am."

"Don't laugh at her, children. Explain. Show her what to do."

Miss Betty wasn't so bad really. But she was impatient and there were so many things to learn.

The only thing that reminded her of home was the large lot beside them. It was covered with bushes and weeds of all sorts and had several large fruit trees on which the neighbourhood feasted. The lot was large enough to hold three or four houses like Miss Betty's.

It was a shame, Sylvie had heard Miss Betty and her husband complaining. The area was opening up so nicely, but this large lot with its overgrown bushes and trees quite spoiled the neighbourhood with its neat houses in rows and their tidy gardens.

At the corner of the lot furthest away from Miss Betty was an old wooden house in which an oldish woman lived. Nobody was quite sure whether she owned the lot or if she was merely the caretaker.

She spent most of her time trying to police the place and prevent people from stealing the mangoes and pears, guineps, guavas and ackees, for she made her living selling the fruits to higglers.

However, her only weapon was a very loud, shrill voice.

When the ackee trees in particular were ready to be reaped, she would spend half of a day or more sitting among them and cursing loudly to make people know that she was there.

If anyone she knew strolled onto the premises she would curse that person and his or her family and threaten to call the police.

Sometimes the children from the neighbourhood would cautiously enter the premises, call out to her and then run away, taking great delight in the curses she rained on them.

She had a musical way of cursing in her high-pitched voice, repeating phrase after phrase for emphasis as if making up a song.

Once somebody had shouted to her asking her why she had left her house to watch the trees.

Arms akimbo, feet thin but nevertheless strong, she had repeated for a long time:

"A wha' me come up ya fa?
A wha' me come up ya fa?
Fi ketch oonu criminal an' ole tief
That's wha' me come up ya fa!"

So she went on, and on.

Sylvie liked those days when the old woman, Miss Mason was her name, came out with a stool and sat in a clearing between the trees and recited her curses. Sometimes you couldn't see her, only hear her voice.

Miss Betty's children were not allowed to enter this lot. When their ball went into the bushes it was Sylvie who had to climb through the barbed wire fencing the premises and search through broomweed, prickly bushes and tall grass to find it.

It was Sylvie who stole through the fence and picked coolie plums and other delicacies for them.

Miss Betty also sent Sylvie to pick "a dozen or so" ackees whenever she was in need and the trees were bearing.

Sylvie was frightened at the thought of being caught, for Miss Mason constantly threatened to call the police for trespassers.

Over the few months that she had lived with Miss Betty, Sylvie had gone through the fence many times to pick fruits, but she had always made sure that Miss Mason was not around before starting her mission.

Then came the day when there were no open ackees near the ground which the short stick she had could reach, so she went back to tell Miss Betty who was immediately angry.

"But anybody ever see my dying trial? Don't you come from country, girl? Look how much open ackee . on the trees!" she exclaimed, peering from her back-yard at the trees. "Climb the tree, girl. A dozen or so don't take no time to pick."

Sylvie crossed the fence reluctantly. She had never been a good climber. When everybody else nimbly climbed into trees to pick fruits or play, she was usually left on the ground to catch the fruits or fend for herself. Once or twice when she had climbed a tree in the country she had been so terrified of falling that she didn't even mind the other children jeering her and calling her " 'fraidy cat."

Sylvie took her time, half hoping to hear Miss Mason coming as this would give her a good excuse to go back.

No Miss Mason.

Heart in her mouth, she tried to hoist herself up to the lowest limb and was only successful after the third attempt. All in vain as she had left the stick on the ground and had to go back down for it.

Finally she got herself and the stick up to a fairly comfortable limb within reach of the open ackees and nervously began to pick the fruits. She was concentrating so hard on keeping her balance, manoeuvring the stick and trying to keep count of how many she had picked (Miss Betty's dozen or so meant not less than three dozen) that she did not hear the siren in the distance.

Suddenly she was aware of a frightening noise, a great continuous clanging of bells coming nearer and nearer.

Sylvie could not tell what was happening. She didn't know what the noise was about. For a moment she remembered the Bible verse which spoke of the trumpet call at the resurrection.

Jesus help me, she thought.

Then as if the noise was not enough, from her perch in the tree she saw a bright red vehicle coming

"Miss Betty, ooh!"

along the road with strange looking men hanging from the sides. They were dressed in black and wore large hats which almost covered their faces. Indeed she couldn't be sure they were men at all.

Sylvie let go her stick and wrapped herself around the tree.

"Miss Betty! Miss Betty!" she screamed. "Them coming for me, ma'am. Them coming for me!" For the vehicle had stopped and the men had jumped off and were now quickly reeling off a long hose.

Sylvie shut her eyes, she didn't want to see any more.

"Miss Betty! Lawd, a dead now! Our Father which art in heaven. Help, Jesus! Miss Betty, ooh!"

Sylvie screamed and moaned alternately, hugging the tree trunk as if her very life depended on it.

When she felt hands touching her, she opened her eyes, saw the helmeted figure reaching for her and promptly fainted.

When Miss Betty told her husband the story that night he laughed so hard he nearly had a heart attack.

It seemed that Miss Mason had seen Sylvie in the tree and asked somebody to telephone the police for her. There was some misunderstanding, however, and the fire brigade had come instead. Sylvie, screaming her head off in the tree, had obviously been in such difficulty that having ascertained that there was no fire, the men had brought out their ladder and rescued her. They had had to work on her with smelling salts and cold water to bring her around. Whereupon, seeing the several firemen surrounding her, she had dashed to her room and bolted the door. It was several hours before Miss Betty could coax her to come out

61

and then she had been so nervous that she had not been able to do a thing in the house.

Miss Betty had suffered the added indignity of being cursed by Miss Mason for several hours.

Miss Betty told her husband that she was sending Sylvie back to the country, for a girl so foolish was of no use to her.

Sylvie was glad to hear this. Before Miss Betty could change her mind, she was packed and ready.

With no regrets, she said her goodbyes and started the return journey home.

What a lot of things she would have to tell her brothers and sisters! But the worst tale of all – would they believe her? – was about the day the devils came after her.

BEST FRIENDS

Everything conspired against Jezebel: her name, her age, her size. To be a well developed thirteen- or fourteen-year-old (she was not quite sure of her age) in a class of ten-year-olds was one problem. To be thought ugly and dunce made it worse. Besides, her hands and knees were scruffy and blackened with dirty work.

She was the target of every unkind prank the other children could think of. Even the teacher seemed to dislike her, and when anybody wanted to curse somebody else really badly, the curse word was always – Jezebel.

Pinky, on the other hand, was small and cute – fairish, as her pet name suggested, and quite bright. She always came in the top eight in her class. She was particularly good at arithmetic and spelling and often the other children sought her help to complete their homework or explain a problem. And because she could move her small frame swiftly on the playing field, she was always sure of a pick for baseball, catchings, chevy chase or ring games.

Nobody would willingly pick Jezebel. The side had to be extra critically short of a "man" with absolutely nobody else available before she was reluctantly asked to join a game.

It seemed quite strange, therefore, that Pinky and Jezebel should become friends.

But Pinky had a soft heart. Although she didn't say anything when the other children teased Jezebel, she was often very sorry for her. It must be awful, she thought, to be so ugly and so disliked by everybody.

Pinky didn't consciously seek to become friends with Jezebel. It just sort of happened.

Pinky had one weakness and Jezebel had one strength, and this was what brought them together.

Pinky could not sew. She hated needlework class. Somehow the thread always got tangled. Her embroidery patterns always came out askew. She couldn't learn to darn properly. The thimble felt clumsy on her finger and the needle always drew blood at least once during the class. She rarely got more than twenty out of a hundred marks for her work, because she rarely ever finished it. So that at the end of the term when the other girls were proudly taking home their embroidered guest towels and runners for dressing tables, she kept her material crumpled at the bottom of her school bag, well out of sight.

But Jezebel could sew. It was as if the ugliness in her life transformed into beauty when she sewed. Her lines were perfectly straight or curved, just as they were meant to be. Her embroidered birds seemed to lift themselves off the cloth to chirp. Her flowers were so beautiful, you could almost smell them. Words which she could hardly write properly in her exercise book came out properly formed. No design seemed too complicated for her. In sewing class those grime-stained fingers became magic wands stitching beauty into the material.

Jezebel was so skilful, that the teachers in the lower school had taken to bringing their guest towels and pillowcases and aprons and different knick-knacks for her to beautify. They never paid her for her work, but Jezebel didn't seem to mind. As she sewed she forgot the trials of her life, concentrating only on the beauty being fashioned by her fingers.

She was proud of her skill, although none of the other girls seemed unduly impressed, except Pinky.

During needlework class, Miss Adams was not so strict, and the girls were allowed to walk about provided they didn't get too noisy. So one day, frustrated by her inability to smock the piece of cloth on which she was learning, Pinky strolled over to Jezebel who was sitting by herself on the back bench.

Some of the girls looked around in surprise when Pinky sat down. Nobody willingly sat beside Jezebel.

Jezebel, accustomed to her loneliness, was also surprised when Pinky, shy of asking too directly for help, began to talk.

"Who teach you to sew so good?" she asked.

"Nobody," Jezebel answered, tongue-tied at the attention and the praise. "I just know how to do it."

"Your mother sew?"

"I don't have a mother. I live with a lady."

"Oh," said Pinky, surprised. Most children she knew had mothers, even if they didn't have fathers.

"You... you could help me with this pattern?" Pinky asked shyly. Jezebel was even more surprised. From time to time some of the other girls might ask her to finish their work for them, but usually it was a

"Who teach you to sew so good?"

command. "Here. Finish this!" And if she didn't, they would increase their name calling, trying to make life even more miserable for her.

In particular, Jezebel feared the snail trails that she would often find on her desk and chair. She was terrified of snails and, unfortunately for her, the children had discovered this. Every now and then she would come in and see the slimy trails on her desk and she would not be able to sit during class. This got her into all sorts of trouble with the teacher, much to the amusement of her classmates, and she would end up having to clean off the slimy traces while praying that the snail was no longer around.

So it was with a degree of timid pleasure that Jezebel patiently showed Pinky how to hold the cloth and how to gather the material to get the distinctive honeycomb smocking pattern. But Pinky got more and more tangled in her threads, so Jezebel quickly completed two rows for her, with such precision that she was lost in wonder.

"You really can sew!" she said admiringly.

Gradually it became a habit for Pinky to sit beside Jezebel in sewing class and, grateful for her help and guidance, Pinky's sewing even began to improve.

It seemed only natural, therefore, for Pinky to start to help Jezebel with her sums and the other school work which gave her so much trouble.

As Pinky talked to Jezebel over a period she learned much about Jezebel's problems.

She learned that Jezebel's mother had died when she was little and an aunt had taken her in, but when the aunt could no longer keep her, she had sent her to a lady who sent her to school, but not regularly enough for her to learn very much, so she was always backward and left behind, while other children moved up. When she didn't come to school, it was because she had too much housework to do.

Pinky was horrified. She was the child of a poor home herself – "poor but trying" – but no one, certainly not her mother, would ever dream of keeping her out of school, because it was only through education that they would be able to "hold up them head." In fact Pinky often had to attend school even when she wasn't feeling well, for fear that she might "miss something important."

Little by little, Pinky and Jezebel became good friends. Pinky would share the goodies she was able to buy with the little extra money she got from time to time – "back and front," fruits, aerated water, sweets – all the special little nice things that they didn't get with the two-penny lunch at the school canteen.

But the friendship put Pinky in the bad books of the other children, who could not understand how she could want to be friends with Jezebel.

Sometimes Pinky was a little worried about the unkind things the other children said. They had started calling her "Jezebel lover" and "Jezebel twin" and they tried to ostracise her. But the fact that she was bright meant that they couldn't completely ignore her. They very often had to ask her to help them, especially with the problem sums. So Pinky didn't mind too much.

Besides, she found that Jezebel knew a number of interesting things to do and places to go. Left to herself so often, Jezebel had wandered through the roads and lanes around the school and she was able to show Pinky places she had never known about.

As soon as they had finished the school lunch (sometimes they used the twopence to buy bulla and cheese at the Chinese shop instead) they would wander about the streets for the rest of the lunch break. Jezebel had learned the exact amount of time that they needed to be able to roam and then make their way back to school, so that they were very rarely late for the afternoon session.

One gloriously sunny afternoon they didn't return at all. That was the afternoon that some very important person was being buried in the cathedral nearby and they had stayed to watch all the cars and the hearse and the many dressed-up people who attended the service and burial in the churchyard.

Jezebel showed Pinky the most exciting places. Like the yard where a murder had been committed. Jezebel didn't say when it had happened, but Pinky gazed with fascination into the yard almost as if she was expecting to see the murder scene re-enacted before her.

Best of all she liked when they roamed through the churchyard. The burial ground with the very fancy tombstones frightened her in a pleasing sort of way. She was afraid of the ghosts, but she liked to examine the carvings and read the headstones, much to Jezebel's annoyance. She was bored by this and wanted to move on to the other side of the cemetery where there were mango and plum trees to stone.

One day they ventured into the cathedral itself. Neither of them was a Catholic and they were a bit awed by the grandeur of the church, but they decided to follow the two old ladies and copy whatever they did. So they dipped their fingers in the holy water in the font at the entrance and made the sign of the cross on their foreheads then wandered inside the church.

Pinky was struck by the beauty of the stained windows and the many statues and the dressed-up altar.

One gloriously sunny afternoon, they didn't return to school

It was so different from her own church which seemed quite plain and unexciting in comparison. She would have liked to stand and gaze, but Jezebel stuck her in the side with her elbow to remind her that they were supposed to be following what the old women were doing.

The women were in fact genuflecting before the statues on their way to the altar.

Jezebel and Pinky tried to bend their knees and bow their heads like the women, but at the second statue Pinky, looking around at her friend, found that she looked so clumsy that she couldn't help giggling.

Instantly, an outraged "shh!" sounded through the church. But this only made them want to giggle more; so, overcome with laughter, they fled the premises.

But the times with Jezebel were not all spent in exploration and laughter. Little by little as the friendship progressed, Pinky learned more and more about how difficult life was for Jezebel.

She learned how Jezebel hated to be thought ugly and dunce. How she had set her heart on being a postmistress like her mother who had died, and that was why she continued to try to come to school although everything was so difficult.

Pinky learned how much the teasing by the other children hurt Jezebel. This she understood fully as she was now sometimes included in the teasing and on the days when Jezebel was absent she would often be alone.

Pinky, however, was able to tell Jezebel that the snail trails which Jezebel saw on her desk were not actually made by snails since the other children were

Overcome with laughter, they fled the premises

themselves afraid of snails. What they did was to cut off a piece of the cactus growing at the end of the school yard and use the slime it produced to make the trails.

But Jezebel's most bitter complaint was the fact that always she was singled out to do the dirty work.

At home she had to use red dye to clean the floor on Saturdays and she never could get her hands and knees clean, no matter how many cut limes she used to rub them.

At school, if the teacher came in and found the classroom dirty it was she who was sent to fetch the broom and sweep out the dirt.

But worst of all, Jezebel confided, was the time when one of the girls vomited in the classroom and she had been sent for the bucket and mop to clean it up. Apart from the bad smell, some of it touched her hand and had felt slimy just like a snail. This had affected her so badly that even in telling Pinky about it, she began to twitch with anger. But, she said, she had learned that people treated her even worse when she objected to the things they asked her to do.

Pinky was so sorry for Jezebel. If she could, she would have liked to prevent life being so difficult for her. But although she didn't realise it, Pinky's friendship was a shining light in Jezebel's life.

Because of Pinky, she made an even greater effort not to be absent from school. She tried to be neater, combing her short hair in smaller plaits so they stayed in place. She tried harder with school work so that a small improvement was noticed by the teacher. As much as the teacher thought the friendship strange,

73

for some reason it seemed to be helping both girls and she could not but admire Pinky's compassion and courage in befriending the outcast. In time, some of the other children even stopped being so horrible to Jezebel.

Then one day Pinky arrived at school feeling sick. She had begged her mother not to send her to school, but as usual her mother had insisted. After all, she might "miss something important."

It was during English composition class that the catastrophe happened. Miss Adams was a strict teacher who rarely allowed a child to go outside during class time. She insisted that they should discipline themselves and "do their business" during break and lunch time. So that any child with an urgent call had almost to meet disaster before she would be given permission to go out.

Pinky, feeling sicker by the minute, felt her stomach turn over in the first movement towards vomiting.

"Please, Miss," she said anxiously, putting up her hand.

"What is it, Maureen?" (Pinky's right name).

"Please, Miss," she said again anxiously, placing her hand over her mouth.

"Speak up," Miss Adams replied, but it was too late. Vomit spewed through her fingers, seeming to project itself more, the greater her effort to contain it.

The desk which she shared with Jezebel, the bench, the floor, everything was covered with her shame, and the girls were scornfully pulling away.

Panic-stricken, she raced from the classroom leaving a trail of vomit behind. She rushed to the bath-

"Please, Miss!"

room to vent herself of the poison in her system. The
class monitor followed to help her, as was the custom.

When she was washing her hands and her face at
the basin and trying to clean the vomit off her uni-
form, she suddenly remembered the dirty classroom.

"I must get the bucket," she said, weakly.

"Don't worry," the monitor said. "Jezebel will clean
it up."

"No!" Pinky insisted. Although she was feeling weak and sick she didn't want Jezebel to do it. She remembered too clearly all the things Jezebel had told her.

"Cho! What you worrying about. No you friend? That's all she good for anyway," the other girl said.

Pinky said nothing. Then they turned around to see Jezebel with the bucket and mop at the door. The look of betrayal on her face, Pinky would remember to the end of her days.

"Jezebel!" she cried, but the other girl had turned away and she was feeling too sick to make the effort to detain her.

Tomorrow, she thought, as they led her to the sick room. She would talk to Jezebel tomorrow and make matters right.

But it was nearly three weeks before she could go back to school. Her upset that day had signalled the start of an attack of measles.

When Pinky returned to school she didn't see Jezebel, and since she sometimes stayed away from school, Pinky didn't worry. One week later, however, when Jezebel had still not turned up, Pinky went to Miss Adams to ask her if she knew what had happened to her.

"Who knows?" Miss Adams replied. "It seems that she has decided to stop for good, this time. Come to think of it," she said, "I haven't seen her since that day you were sick and I sent her to clean up the classroom. She started mopping the floor and then suddenly left the bucket and mop and walked out. I had to send for the janitor and interrupt the class until it was all cleaned."

"Jezebel! Jezebel!"

Pinky was sad. She felt even worse when she realised that as much as they had talked, she didn't even know Jezebel's address. And even if she knew it her mother would not have allowed her to visit. Perhaps, though, she could have written her. She missed Jezebel a lot for the rest of the time she spent in Standard Four.

Pinky saw Jezebel only once more after that.

One day, many months later, she was downtown waiting for a bus and Jezebel passed by laden with a basket of foodstuff. She was obviously coming from the market.

"Jezebel! Jezebel!" Pinky cried excitedly.

Jezebel turned around, looked at her fully and then walked on without a sign of recognition.

CHAMPION

"Champion coming! Champion coming!"
The news would spread fast and the children would quickly leave what they were doing to peep over the walls or through fences and windows or to join Champion as he progressed half-drunk down the lane to his favourite bar on the corner.

For Champion could always be counted on to provide entertainment.

He was a lane personality, one of several whose peculiarities made lane life a colourful and sometimes exciting experience.

"Champion a sojer-man! Champion a sojer-man!" they would chant if that was his manner of dress for the day; and the bold among them would pretend to shoot at him and he would obligingly return the shots.

"Bang! Bang!" he would shout at them, for he was always tolerant and kind to the children.

Champion had a bad "sorefoot." Not that you ever saw the sore itself, but the foot was always swollen and always bandaged near the ankle. This foot could only fit into an old slipper. His "sam platters" he called it. On the good foot he wore a black shoe and sock always. If you could only see his feet you would swear that you were looking at the feet of two different people.

"Champion coming! Champion coming!"

And that was how Champion behaved anyway –
like two different people. The Champion who didn't
drink was a quiet, pleasant, middle-aged man. The
Champion who drank was alternately a wild cowboy,
rakish film star, bullfighter, soldier, sailor, politician or
one of several other personalities.

He improvised different costumes to emphasise
these roles, utilising bath towels, old hats or caps, an
old coat or two; he even had a scissors-tail coat and
an old rat-chewed top hat. Various shabby scarves
and an old pair of spectacles helped out on occasion,
and invariably the costume was completed by the
glass of "whites" in his hand – he always carried his
own glass to the bar.

The merriment would increase as he made his way
down the lane acting out his role for that day.

"One, two, three, four
Colon man a come
With him brass chain
A lick him belly
Bam! bam! bam!"

– the lane children would sing as they followed him.

But the most exciting role for them was that of
bullfighter.

"Toro! Toro!" he would shout at the head of the
lane, and the children would come running.

"Bullfighter! Bullfighter! See the bull ya, Mr.
Champion. Bull! Bull!" they would shout, scampering
around him, and Champion would obligingly wave his
red towel at them.

81

"See the bull ya, Mr. Champion!"

Then they would run about and shout with glee, round and round, repeating their cries until he reached the bar and disappeared inside. Even then they would hang about because sometimes he would reappear to give another demonstration.

The adults, irritated by Champion's foolishness,

would warn the children to leave him alone, but they just couldn't resist him.

But Babs was afraid of Mr. Champion.

The problem was that he lived in her yard, in a room at the back with the woman who looked after him. They called her "Missis Champion" although Champion was not his real name. They said that he had been a boxer in his youth and that was how he got the name. Mr. Champion, it seemed, had done a great many things in his life.

He didn't go to the rum shop every day, for Missis Champion kept a stern eye on him, but since she had to go out to tend to her higglering business he had plenty of opportunity to indulge in his whims and fantasies.

She would leave him at home nursing his "sorefoot" and complaining to anyone who would listen about how he had "come down in the world." Life, it seemed, had treated him cruelly. In his time he had been policeman, canecutter, boxer, conductor. Many were the careers he had followed in strange lands, so he said.

Champion also had a bad cough. He would sit and hack for minutes at a time. The only thing which relieved his cough, he said, was the little "whites."

Sometimes Babs and some other children in the yard got together and sang the songs they learned at school. One of their favourites was "John Brown's Baby."

"John Brown baby have a cold upon him chest
Rub it with some camphorated oil."

Before they reached the "Glory, glory, Hallelujah" part, Babs would begin to think of Mr. Champion with sadness. This song always reminded her of him sitting at his doorstep nursing his lame foot and coughing and coughing.

She wondered if Missis Champion knew about camphorated oil, but she knew better than to ask such a question. Children didn't get mixed up in big people's business. So she kept as far away from Mr. Champion as she could, both afraid of and sorry for him.

Champion would go on a binge soon after one of his sons visited. Missis Champion never gave him money since she knew he would only spend it on rum. Neither did his daughter. But his sons could always be counted on to leave a "little something" with the old man when they visited him.

As soon as the son left, Champion would seek out a child in the yard to send to the shop for a "Q." He had a special flask which he hid from Missis Champion and he would give the child two shillings with instructions that Miss Sally at the corner shop should be told that Champion needed a "li'l something for the cough."

Children weren't allowed into the bar so Miss Sally or whoever else was selling in the shop would go into the bar and return the bottle three quarters full.

One day Babs was the only child in the yard and Champion asked her to go to the shop for him. She didn't want to go, but children couldn't refuse any reasonable request made by an adult, and while her mother did not like her going to the shop to buy rum for Mr. Champion, Babs knew that if he complained she would be publicly berated for not running the errand. Because if she wasn't scolded they would be accused of "thinking them better than other people," and there would be no peace for them in the yard after that.

So Babs reluctantly went to the shop.

It was while she was returning from the shop that Babs got a brilliant idea.

Mr. Champion obviously needed something stronger than rum for his cough. If rubbing him with camphorated oil helped John Brown's baby, perhaps it would help Mr. Champion too. She didn't have camphorated oil, but her mother kept some camphor balls soaking in white rum which she used to rub her pains, and her feet if they got wet. So Babs made a brief detour.

Champion, thirsty for his drink, checked neither look nor smell when Babs brought him his flask. He threw back his head and poured the contents into his mouth.

The look of choking surprise, the hand clutching the throat, and the frenzied jig forgetful even of the lame foot so alarmed Babs that she started to run even before she heard the first cries of "Murda! Police! Pizen!"

By the time the crowd gathered around Champion, Babs was halfway up the lane, running along the path which her mother usually took from work.

It was night before Babs, frightened to death, returned to the yard with her mother.

Not a word would she say, and her mother, who had been surprised to find her waiting on the street, was worried about her strange behaviour.

Babs sat quietly in the room. The yard itself was

85

"Murda! Police! Pizen!"

ominously silent. Silence with a waiting-to-explode feeling in it.

Nobody spoke to Babs or her mother. Not at the standpipe. Not even a "good evening" as she cooked their dinner in the coal pot outside the door.

Wise in the ways of yards, Babs's mother put the strange behaviour of her daughter together with the strange behaviour of the yard and came up with the right answer.

"What happen here today?" she enquired sternly of the silent Babs. "What you do?"

But Babs only shook her head, unable to speak.

So they sat at their little table on the verandah pretending to eat. Presently a harsh voice began to shout.

"Mistress Adassa! A word with you, ma'am."

The tone of voice and the words of address signalled the ultimate in battle cries.

"What is it, Missis Champion?" Babs's mother replied, trying to sound placatory.

"I want you to know that you harbouring a criminal in you house. You daughter nearly kill mi husband this morning. Is only the mercy of God why him is still alive. She gi' him poison fi drink an' all now him still suffering. Him admit an' is groaning in hospital bed in Public, barely alive."

She didn't add that the effect of the camphorated rum had not lasted too long since Champion had sputtered out most of it, but that on arrival at the hospital the doctor was more interested in his bad foot and that was why he was detained.

Babs's mother clutched her heart at the news and Babs herself nearly fainted from fright.

"Mistress Adassa! A word with you, ma'am."

Missis Champion didn't stop there, she went on to trace the generation of murderers from which Babs was descended and promised that the police would be coming for her.

When she was satisfied she went away and the yard held its breath again, waiting for the second act.

It didn't have long to wait. Mistress Adassa, full of shame, fright, disappointment in her daughter, and frustration from having to put up with Missis Champion's tracing, gave full vent to her feelings by giving Babs a sound beating. Her wails brought a measure of satisfaction to the yard.

No police really came, but they didn't wait to find out.

Next morning when the yard woke up, Babs's room was locked up tight.

The yard never saw Babs again, and Mistress Adassa only once, when she came with the handcart man to remove her belongings to wherever it was that she was making a new home for herself and her daughter.

HURRICANE CHARLIE

The next day when Kenneth saw the destruction, he was glad that his name was not Charlie. Any boy named Charlie would be in for serious teasing when he returned to school the following month.

Hurricane Charlie was a big one with winds up to one hundred and twenty miles an hour. It was hard to imagine wind travelling so fast. Faster than the fastest car he had ever seen. Fast like an aeroplane? he wondered. It was hard to imagine wind that was solid like a bulldozer, but that was what seemed to have travelled through the land, knocking down everything or almost everything in its path.

The evidence was all around him. The houses in the tenement yard next door were totally destroyed. Twisted zinc sheets were strewn around and mattresses, pots and pans, clothing and personal belongings floated in the water, inches high, in the yard. The shop down the road had been split in two. The zinc on the roof at the back of his house had lifted, but they had been lucky that it had not been blown off. Only the stalk of the little mango tree was left standing in his yard. The pear tree was lying on its side, roots in the air, the young pears scattered all over. The coconut tree now made a bridge across the yard. The fowl coop was at the far corner, cotched up against the remains of the

90

It seemed that a bulldozer had travelled through the land

fence. Two dead chickens were in it. The rest were walking around, rather hopping about, in the water, with feathers so wet that most of their white skin was showing. Mama said that they would have to eat the chickens before they caught cold and died.

It seemed that most of the trees on the road had been blown down and somebody had reported that the bridge which linked them to the main road had been washed away. Kenneth was waiting on a chance to slip away to see this. The gully would be a raging torrent, he knew. In the light drizzle which was now all that remained of the storm, it was difficult to believe that so much had happened during the night.

At first, Kenneth had not taken the warnings seriously. The neighbours had kept on calling to his mother or sisters to find out what the radio said, the "latest bulletin," they called it. He had been sent to the shop to buy kerosene oil, sardines, bully beef, bread, crackers, condensed milk, all sorts of groceries, although it wasn't Saturday. He thought it strange that they should be buying so many extra things.

Mama and the girls had been in a flurry of activity, washing and drying clothes, because Mama said that she didn't know when she might be able to wash again.

But things only began to look serious after Father came home from work at midday. Most business places had been locked up, he reported, and the workers sent home to prepare for the hurricane. He changed his clothes and then set about pulling out boards and things from under the cellar – and Kenneth was kept busy helping him to batten down the house.

They put pieces of plywood over the glass windows and nailed heavy strips of wood across to keep them in place. Father put on two extra bolts on the front

92

They nailed wood over the windows

and back doors. He nailed the side door shut. They would use only the front or the back door if they had to get out, he said. They never could tell in what direction they might have to run if the house didn't stand up to the wind.

That was the first time that Kenneth began to feel a little worried. He didn't really know what a hurricane was except that Mama had said "Plenty wind and plenty rain." This hadn't sounded frightening, but here was Father talking about the house being blown down. Could any wind be that strong?

For a time, he shared his sisters' excitement as the tempo of preparations increased. But after a while he grew tired of fetching and carrying and holding nails and hammer and pieces of wood. Besides, Mama kept calling him to help her and the girls. He had to help clean out the two drums and fill them with water.

Kenneth sighed as he watched the hose filling the drum. He could hear the boys playing cricket up the street and his feet ached to run away and join them. Although Mama didn't approve (she called them raga-muffin boys) he could sometimes sneak away and get in a game or two before she missed him.

It embarrassed him how she thought that they were better than the other people who lived on their street. Just because their house was a new concrete nog that she had scraped and sacrificed to build (it wasn't even finished yet) instead of board or wattle. They even had a radio, a pretty, shiny wooden box that Father had bought from a man at the wharf. Mama was always listening to some funny programmes on it, "Linda's First Love" and one called "Doctor Paul."

Mama thought things like that important. Things like her drawing room couch and chairs. And she insisted that her children should behave according to their station. She would wink an eye sometimes when he escaped to play "since he was a boy," she said, but the girls could only play when their cousins came to visit. Sometimes he was sorry for them, except that they didn't seem to mind since they also behaved in the same prim and proper way as Mama did, especially Cynthia now that she was thirteen.

Kenneth sighed again as he heard the boys cheering. Somebody must have hit a six. Maybe Stanley, he was good. He hoped it was a safe six that wouldn't get them into trouble.

Today he wouldn't get a chance to sneak away. He knew it. Before he had finished one job somebody was calling him to do another.

"Ken! Remind Father about the chicken coop. He suppose to lash it to the pear tree."

"The drum full up yet? Full the bathpan too and put the bleaching zinc on it with two big stone. The radio say to catch as much water as possible."

"Ken! Kenneth! But where the boy gone to now? Ken! Come, go back to shop for me. I forget the extra matches."

By five o'clock Kenneth was worn out and grumpy as he ate his dinner. Only his family seemed so serious about this hurricane business, he thought.

Everybody else seemed to be treating it like a holiday. When he went to the shop in the square, he had seen the men gathered in little groups chatting. Since everybody was home early, several games of dominoes

Several games of dominoes were going on

were going on in the yards, and at the bar some men were joking that that was where they intended to batten down for the night.

Besides, apart from a redness in the sky and the extra heat because the house was locked up so tight, the day was progressing normally. Not even a little breeze, much less one strong enough to blow down a house.

"The radio say it going to reach between seven and nine o'clock," Mama reported.

Kenneth thought that they were only allowing the radio to frighten them. The women were over-reacting as usual, he was sure. Tired from the day's activities, he went to bed early.

It seemed to Kenneth that he had only just shut his eyes after tossing around restlessly, trying to get comfortable in the heat, when somebody in the kitchen started crashing pots and pans so loudly that it disturbed him. He was wondering who it could be when he heard his mother calling him and realised that he must have been dreaming, for the noise was not coming from the kitchen but outside the house: on the zinc roof, rain like horses' hooves, and crashing and banging from the worst kind of lightning and thunder he had ever heard.

"Ken, wake up," Mama shook him, and he could hear the fear in her voice. "The storm really bad. I don't know what going to happen."

The eerie shadows cast by the lantern she carried were scary.

"Electricity gone," she said, and Kenneth shivered although he wasn't cold.

"Come! Everybody in the drawing room. Is best we stay together in case anything happen."

Kenneth followed her into the drawing room where he saw Father standing before the boarded-up windows, as if he was Superman with x-ray eyes, trying to see what was happening outside.

Cynthia, his older sister, was sitting with an open book before her although Kenneth knew that she couldn't be reading. Mama didn't allow them to spoil their eyes by reading when the light was too dim.

"Ken, wake up."

Lorna, who came between him and Cynthia, looked at him sleepily. She was sitting on the floor with her head on a cushion, leaning against the couch. Every time the lightning crackled and the thunder crashed, shaking the house like an earthquake, she put the cushion over her head.

"Biting ants still scurrying around," Mama said. "Why you don't sit on the couch?" Mama didn't approve of unladylike behaviour, like sitting on the floor, even for ten-year-old girls.

But she didn't have the time to insist for just then a tearing sound, followed by a terrible inhuman groaning and creaking as if seven devils were loose outside, frightened them all into round-eyed silence.

"I wonder what gone now!" Father exclaimed. "I fretting 'bout the kitchen zinc. The damn half-inch carpenter never put it on good, and it don't even seal yet."

"Walter!" Mama scolded. "This is no time to be swearing. Lawd have mercy on us! I fretting 'bout the whole house. The Lord see and know how we sacrifice to build this roof over we head. Protect us this night, oh Jesus!"

Kenneth sat bright-eyed, sleep forgotten, as the storm attacked the house. He imagined it like wicked giant fingers seeking an opening to tear things apart, to rip out the nails he and Father had hammered in, ripping, slashing, tearing to get at them and cast them out into the savage night.

The lightning was so bright that it came through every tiny crack in the windows and doors; the thunder so loud that it made the house shudder time after time. In the back something was slapping against the house. Probably a sheet of zinc, Father said.

Once or twice they thought they heard shouts and wailing, but there was no way of telling if it wasn't just another sound of the wind rushing through some new opening.

Suddenly the noise began to wane and soon all they could hear was the sound of light rain on the roof.

"It done! It stop!" Kenneth's voice sounded loud now that the noise outside had abated.

Father shook his head. "We mus' be reach the eye now."

"I going to take a look outside."

"The eye?"

"You don't know nothing?" Cynthia said in the insulting way she sometimes talked to him. Just because he was the youngest and only nine years old. "The eye is the centre. It always calm. No wind don't blow when it passing. So the radio say."

If it wasn't for the radio, Cynthia wouldn't know anything, Kenneth thought crossly, but forgot her rudeness when Father said, "I going to take a look outside."

"I can go?" Kenneth asked hopefully.

"Just stay where you is," Mama commanded. "Walter, you be careful. The radio say you don't know when it going to start again."

Outside it was now strangely quiet. All they could hear was the swishing of water in the yard.

"It's a good thing the house is high up," Mama said. "It sound like a flood out there."

"The cement under the house mus' be spoil," Father said. "I never remember it."

Carrying the lantern, they followed him down the passage and through the dining room and kitchen to the back door. Water from leaks covered the floor and had soaked the dining table and chairs. When Father tried to open the back door he couldn't, for something heavy was blocking it.

"The pear tree mus' be fall down. That mus' be what we hear a while back," he said.

They trooped back to the drawing room to try the front door.

As Father was about to pull the bolt they heard a loud banging on the other side.

"Mistress! Mistress! Let we in. Do!"

Here was a new fright to add to the night's woes.

"Wonder who...?" Mama said.

They all held their breath as Father pulled the bolts on the double door and carefully half-opened one side.

"Who out there?" Father called.

"Is me, Beatrice, sar."

Father opened the door and Kenneth recognised

the woman who lived in the front room next door. She was soaked and shivering, and pieces of leaves and mud were stuck to her clothing. She was carrying a bundle which looked like it contained a baby. In her other hand she carried a small boy, soaked through.

"Do sar, let we in. The house blow 'way."

Father didn't need to be urged. He took the child off her hip and helped her into the house.

"What happen?" he asked.

"The roof blow off and zinc start fly all round an' we had was to run! I run to Uncle shop, an' it blow 'way too and all now I don't know what happen to the rest."

As Father was about to close the door, they heard a shout. Hurrying to the door came Uncle, the man who kept the little shop down the road.

"A glad fi see you light. A didn't know which way a was going." He was followed by Mac, the boy who helped in the shop.

"Lawd, Beatrice," he exclaimed when he saw her, "a glad you safe! So much water 'pon the road, me nearly wash 'way."

Uncle's forehead had a gash in the middle with bloody water oozing from it. A limb from a guinep tree had split the shop in two, and he had been cut by a piece of board.

"Lawd, have mercy!" Mama exclaimed when she saw him.

There was now almost total confusion in the drawing room. Cynthia and Lorna were helping Beatrice unwrap the baby from the wet blanket. Mama seemed flustered. Kenneth saw her hesitate and realised that she was having a small argument with her "station in

102

Uncle's forehead had a gash

life." But only for a moment, then she took Beatrice and the wet children into her bedroom.

Soon she was back with a towel and two of Father's shirts for Uncle and Mac. She couldn't find anything to put on Uncle's cut except Thermogene Medicated Rub.

Kenneth stared in fascination at Uncle. He knew Thermogene could burn. How could Uncle stand that on his cut? But Uncle was too distracted at the loss of his shop and his brush with death to care what was put on the cut.

Mama put on the Thermogene and a weird thing happened. The flesh around the cut suddenly began to swell. Just like a balloon right before their eyes, poof it went, up and up with the gash in the middle like an eye – a red eye. Kenneth stared and stared. He wondered if it would burst.

Mama became even more flustered. She put the damp towel on it and after a while it stopped swelling.

By the time they were all re-assembled in the drawing room the refugees from the storm were a little more comfortable. Mama had found dry clothes for Beatrice, and the little boy had on one of Kenneth's tee shirts. It was too big for him and he looked like a pint-sized clown in a big nightgown.

Father locked and bolted the door and in a little while they heard the wind starting up again.

"It coming from the other side now. What don't blow down yet going to blow down now," Cynthia said. "So the radio say," she added, glaring at Kenneth.

They looked at her fearfully. Some of them had already experienced the horror, others were praying to avoid it.

A feeling of friendliness and warmth passed through Kenneth

Miraculously, it seemed, Mama produced mugs and started sharing hot cocoa from a giant Thermos. Kenneth wondered about this; it was as if she had been expecting visitors. She didn't say anything either when Father suggested that Uncle and Mac needed a tot of something strong in their mugs.

As the storm started blowing again, Mama set about getting blankets and pillows so that those who wanted to do so could lie down. She insisted that they should stay together, "just in case."

Busy settling her guests and family, she forgot to be fearful as she listened to Beatrice's tale of disaster and tried to encourage her not to worry too much about the others who lived in the yard. Papa was talking to Uncle about the shop, Cynthia and Lorna were taking turns holding the baby who was sleeping through all the excitement. The little clown was lying on a blanket; he would soon be asleep. And Mac from the shop was sipping the hot cocoa with the same slightly stupid expression he always wore.

Kenneth looked around and a feeling of friendliness and warmth passed through him. For a while it didn't matter about the violence outside. There was peace and love inside.

Printed in the United States
3592